UNCLE ALPHONSO AND THE
Greedy Green Dinosaurs

Jack Pearson • Terry Julien

Chariot Books™
David C. Cook Publishing Co.

E
PEA

Chariot Books™ is an imprint of David C. Cook Publishing Co.
David C. Cook Publishing Co., Elgin, Illinois 60120
David C. Cook Publishing Co., Weston, Ontario
Nova Distribution Ltd., Torquay, England

UNCLE ALPHONSO AND THE GREEDY GREEN DINOSAURS
©1992 by Jack Pearson for text and Terry Julien for illustrations

Art direction by Randy Maid
First Printing, 1992
Printed in Singapore
96 95 94 93 92   5 4 3 2 1

Library of Congress Cataloging-in-Publication Data
Pearson, Jack,
      Uncle Alphonso and the greedy green dinosaurs/Jack Pearson;
[illustrated by Terry Julien]
      p.   cm - (On my own books)
      Summary: Uncle Alphonso explains to Anna and Nathan how the greed of
the dinosaurs known as Greedogoldfusses, and their lack of faith in God, led to the
downfall of the entire species.
      ISBN 1-55513-424-6
      [1. Greed-- Fiction. 2. Fiction.] 3. Christian life-fiction. 4. Uncles-- Fiction.]
I.Julien, Terry, ill. 11. Title.
PZ7.P323126Un 1991
[E]--dc20   90-20340
                                   CIP

"I'm rich," sang Anna as she teetered on top of the retaining wall. "I've got twenty-one whole dollars in my bank account!"

Her twin brother, Nathan, didn't seem impressed. "Okay, so you've got twenty-one dollars. But you need more than that to be rich."

"No, you don't," protested Anna with a toss of her head. "And I'm going to get even richer, too. When I get big, I'm going to make so much money I'll go swimming in it every day!"

"Yeah. You and the goldfish," Nathan snickered.

"Oooh, Nathan, you're just jealous because you're not rich and I am," snapped Anna.

"Are not."

"Am too!"

"Are not!"

"Am too! I call 'no backs,' and besides, here we are at Uncle Alphonso's house. We'll ask him. He knows what rich is."

Nathan and Anna had stopped at the gate of a wonderful old house down the block from their house. Uncle Alphonso (who was actually the children's great-uncle) lived there with his old furniture, a cat named Teacup, and his study stacked to the ceiling with books and fossils.

Uncle Alphonso was one of Nathan's and Anna's very favorite people. He had retired from teaching at the university, but still worked part-time down at the museum with the dinosaur exhibits. He was one of the world's leading dinosaur experts.

"Now you'll see," said Anna to her brother as she held open the screen door and clunked with the big door knocker.

A large, balding man answered. "Why,
Nathan and Anna. Come in, come in! You must
have smelled the cookies baking."

"No, but could we have one anyway?" asked
Nathan.

"Of course," chuckled the old man holding a
plate within Nathan's eager reach. "And how
about you, Anna?"

"Thank you very much," said Anna, remembering her manners. Then forgetting them again she mumbled with a mouthful of cookies, "Uncle Alph, I've got twenty-one whole dollars, but Nathan doesn't think I'm rich. I am rich, aren't I?"

"Well, well," replied the man thoughtfully. "That
depends. But come on up to the study. There's
something I'd like to show you."

The children were excited because this meant
they would get to see Uncle Alphonso's amazing
fossil collection. There was nothing they liked
half as well. Their great-uncle was famous for
finding funny fossils no one had ever heard of
before. Up the stairs they went and into the study.

"Now then," began the old man as they all seated themselves. "Talk of money like this brings us smack up against one of the greatest fossil discoveries of my career." He opened a large box in the corner and took from it a large, odd-shaped stone.

"It looks like some kind of nest," said Nathan.

"Excellent! Excellent, my boy!" exclaimed Uncle Alphonso. "It is! The only known fossil nest of a rare dinosaur of the bonehead species: the Greedogoldfuss.*"

Teacup, the cat, jumped into his lap as he settled back into his chair.

*greed-o-**gold**-fuss

Anna and Nathan settled in, too. They knew they were in for an interesting story.

"As you may have heard," began Uncle Alphonso, "I taught Boneheadology at the university for many years. The boneheads were a peculiar race of dinosaurs that died out for some very boneheaded reasons. Now take the Greedogoldfuss here. It was a rare type of winged lizard with real money problems!" He reached into the fossil nest and pulled out a round, yellow rock. "Do you kids know what this is?"

Anna and Nathan shook their heads slowly. "Gold," their great-uncle replied. "A solid-gold nest egg. The nest is full of them."

"That's why you call it the . . . the greedy-gold-foot?" asked Anna.

"Exactly, dear girl," replied Uncle Alphonso with a hearty laugh. "The Greedogoldfusses were in love with gold. And they did wear it on their feet, too. Legbands, toe rings, and also necklaces and bracelets. All made from gold they found in the bends of the river. What they couldn't wear, they made into these eggs for their nests."

"I'll bet they looked beautiful," said Anna, who was fond of jewelry.

"Oh, yes. Indeed," replied Uncle Alph. "But they also became terrible show-offs.

"By being greedy they lost most of their friends. The greediest of the Greedogoldfusses had to walk everywhere they went. They wore so much gold that they couldn't fly anymore, you see.

"These creatures may have been boneheads,"
Uncle Alphonso continued, "but they were quite
intelligent in some ways, especially in how they
built their nests. They were the first ones to
think of making them in tree branches

overhanging a river. It kept them safe from
enemies, and also gave them a great view."

"I'll bet the gold got pretty heavy in those
nests," said Nathan as he tested the weight of
one of the eggs in his hand.

"It certainly did, Nathan," replied Uncle Alph. "With each passing year, the gold increased and the tree limbs began to sag under the weight of the Greedogoldfuss nests.

"One evening, a fierce wind storm swept through the river canyon. The trees all groaned and swayed. One by one the branches with the Greedogoldfuss nests in them cracked off and fell into the river far below. What a splash!"

"That's too bad about the nests, Uncle Alph,"
said Anna, "but what happened to the
Greedogoldfusses themselves? Couldn't they live
somewhere else?"

"Ah," said the old man with a sigh. "That's
the saddest part of the story. The creatures
might have survived if they hadn't all jumped
into the river to save their nest eggs.

"They were so weighted down with their golden ornaments, they all promptly drowned, and that was the end of them."

The silence was broken only by Teacup's purring as Uncle Alphonso scratched her ears. Anna and Nathan stared at each other. Finally Nathan spoke. "Sounds like those Greedogoldfusses could have used some swimming lessons!"

"Or a lot less gold," added Anna.

"Or a little more faith!" said Uncle Alph. "That's what really made them boneheads, you know."

"What do you mean?" asked Anna.

"Well, God tells us we should love Him with everything we are, Anna. That's the only road to life. When money or anything else becomes more important than God, then we're headed in the wrong direction."

"I see what you mean," said Anna,

glancing at the fossil nest. "Those Greedogoldfusses were like people who love gold more than God."

"Exactly."

After a brief pause Anna turned to her great-uncle. "I don't think I want to be rich, Uncle Alph."

The old man smiled. "I think twenty-one whole dollars is a lot of money, Anna. Use it wisely. But I also think that it's time for you two to get back to your own little nest. Boneheadology dismissed!"

The children waved as they closed the gate in front of the house. They were part way down the block when Uncle Alphonso called out from the porch, "And say hello to your mother!"